# MINECRAFT
# BLACK PLASMA
# ADVENTURES

THIS IS A MORTIMER CHILDREN'S BOOK
Design © Welbeck Publishing Limited 2020
Published in 2020 by Mortimer Children's Books Limited
An imprint of the Welbeck Publishing Group
20 Mortimer Street, London W1T 3JW

A catalogue record for this book is available from the British Library.

ISBN 978 1 83935 003 0
Printed in China

10 9 8 7 6 5 4 3 2 1

Creator: David Zoellner
Script: Mark Clapham
Special Consultant: Beau Chance
Design: Darren Jordan/Rockjaw Creative, Sam James
Design Manager: Matt Drew
Editorial Manager: Joff Brown
Production: Nicola Davey

# MINECRAFT
# BLACK PLASMA
# ADVENTURES

## 6 HILARIOUS, ACTION-PACKED COMIC BOOK STORIES!

BY
### DAVID ZOELLNER, AKA ARBITER 617

MORTIMER

# ABOUT THE CREATORS

DAVID ZOELLNER, BETTER KNOWN AS ARBITER 617, PLUS HIS COLLEAGUES SAM, KNIGHT AND SKYFALL, ARE ALL PART OF BLACK PLASMA STUDIOS, THE BLOCKBUSTER INTERNET ANIMATION POWERHOUSE WHICH HAS CREATED VIDEOS WITH OVER 32 MILLION VIEWS.

# DERP IN...
# DON'T TOUCH

A REMOTE CAVE, ACCESSIBLE ONLY TO THE BRAVEST OF ADVENTURERS...

... OR ANYONE WITH A MAP!

A CAVE CONTAINING AN INCREDIBLE SECRET.

HMM... WHAT'S THIS?

DERP CAN'T RESIST A SWITCH...

Do not touch!

DERP LOOKS AROUND TO SEE IF ANYONE IS WATCHING...

WHAT HARM COULD IT DO?

CLICK

DERP RUNS TO SAFETY...

... BUT THE SWITCH DOESN'T SEEM DO ANYTHING.

UNTIL GRAVITY GOES INTO REVERSE! DERP IS THROWN INTO THE AIR -

- AND HITS THE CEILING!

FROM DERP'S PERSPECTIVE **UP** IS NOW **DOWN**, SO HE WALKS ACROSS THE CEILING TO SEE...

... HOW FAR THIS CHANGE IN GRAVITY HAS SPREAD.

GRAVITY IS GOING HAYWIRE EVERYWHERE!

EVERYTHING IS UP IN THE AIR.

SOME DON'T LET IT DISTURB THEIR SLEEP...

...WHILE OTHERS HAVE A LESS RESTFUL NIGHT.

DUELS ARE DISRUPTED AT THE MOST AWKWARD MOMENT.

WHILE SOME PEOPLE ARE TRYING TO HOLD ON TO WHAT THEY'VE GOT.

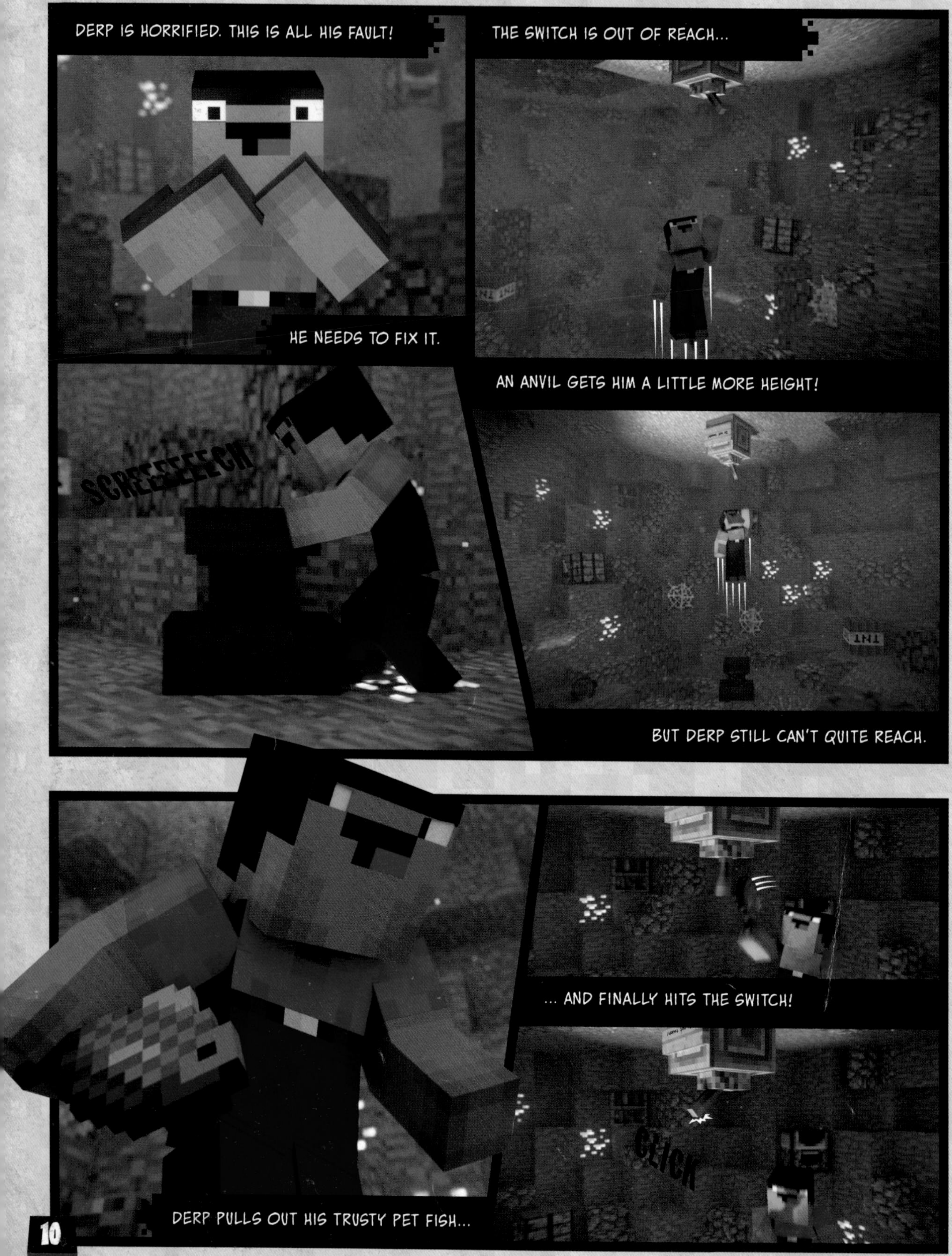
DERP IS HORRIFIED. THIS IS ALL HIS FAULT!
HE NEEDS TO FIX IT.
THE SWITCH IS OUT OF REACH...
SCREEEEECH
AN ANVIL GETS HIM A LITTLE MORE HEIGHT!
TNT
BUT DERP STILL CAN'T QUITE REACH.
DERP PULLS OUT HIS TRUSTY PET FISH...
... AND FINALLY HITS THE SWITCH!
CLICK

WHAT GOES UP MUST COME DOWN...

INCLUDING DERP...

... AND THE ANVIL!

NOW DERP CAN'T REACH THE SWITCH!

THANKFULLY, HELP IS AT HAND.

AS THE OLD MAN SLOOOOWLY REACHES FOR THE SWITCH...

DERP HOLDS HIS BREATH.

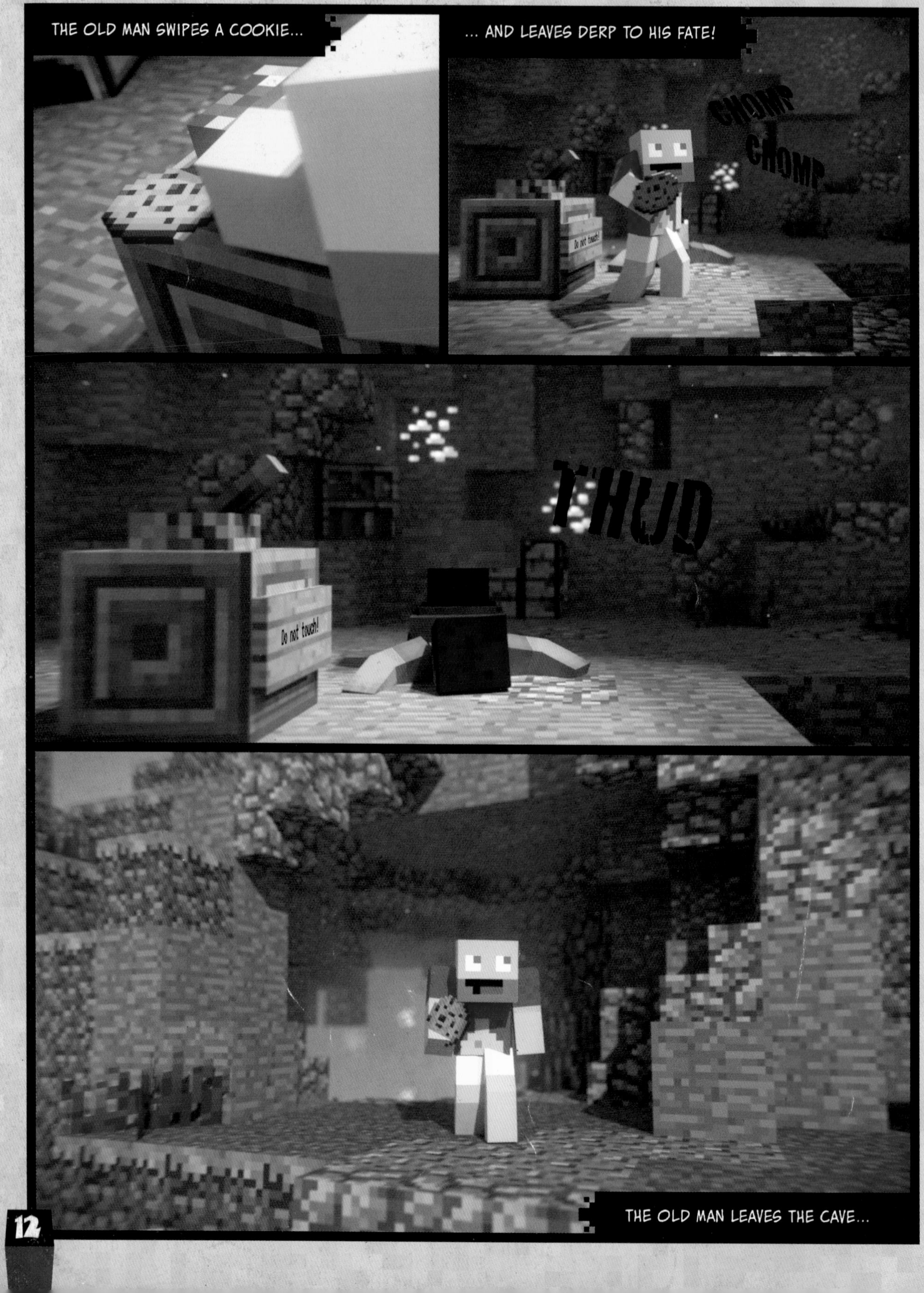
THE OLD MAN SWIPES A COOKIE...
... AND LEAVES DERP TO HIS FATE!
CHOMP
CHOMP
Do not touch!
THUD
Do not touch!
THE OLD MAN LEAVES THE CAVE...

...ONLY FOR ANOTHER SWITCH TO CATCH HIS EYE.

Definitely
Do not touch!

WHAT HARM COULD IT DO?

Definitely
Do not touch!

CLICK

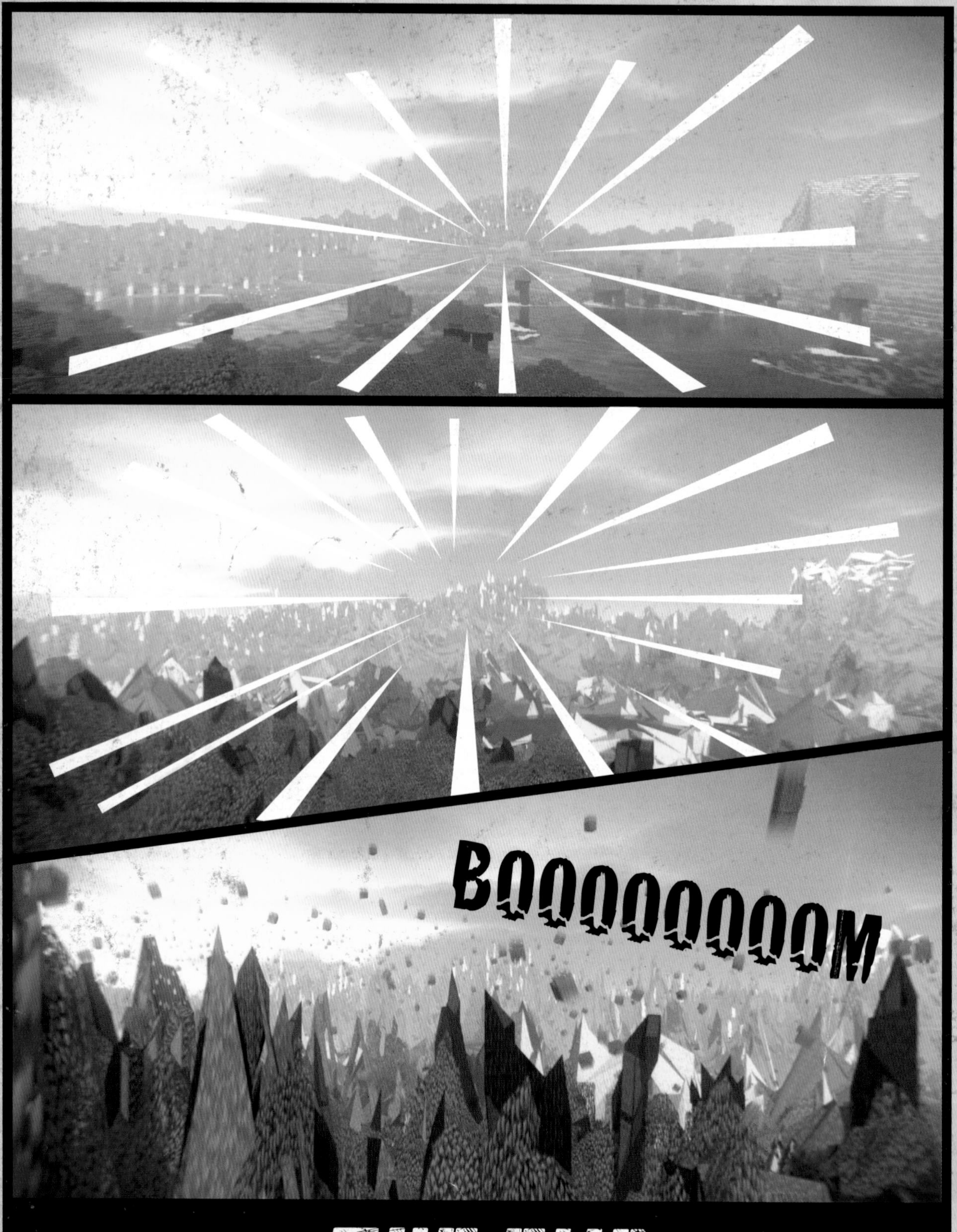
BOOOOOOOOM
THE END

# ZOMBIES

WHAT'S THAT SOUND?

GRRRRR

GRRRRR

SMASH

UH OH! THIS MUST BE A ZOMBIE ATTACK MINIGAME!

THE MISSION: SURVIVE THE WAVES OF INCOMING ZOMBIES.

PISTOLS BLAZE AS THIS TEAM ARE SURROUNDED.

BLADE MEETS AXE IN CLOSE COMBAT!

WITH THE LAST ZOMBIE DOWN...

...THE TEAM MOVE ON TO THE NEXT ROOM.

GRRRRRR

BUT YOU SHOULD NEVER LEAVE A MAN BEHIND...

...JUST IN CASE AN ENEMY ISN'T AS DEAD AS YOU THOUGHT!

ONE DOWN.

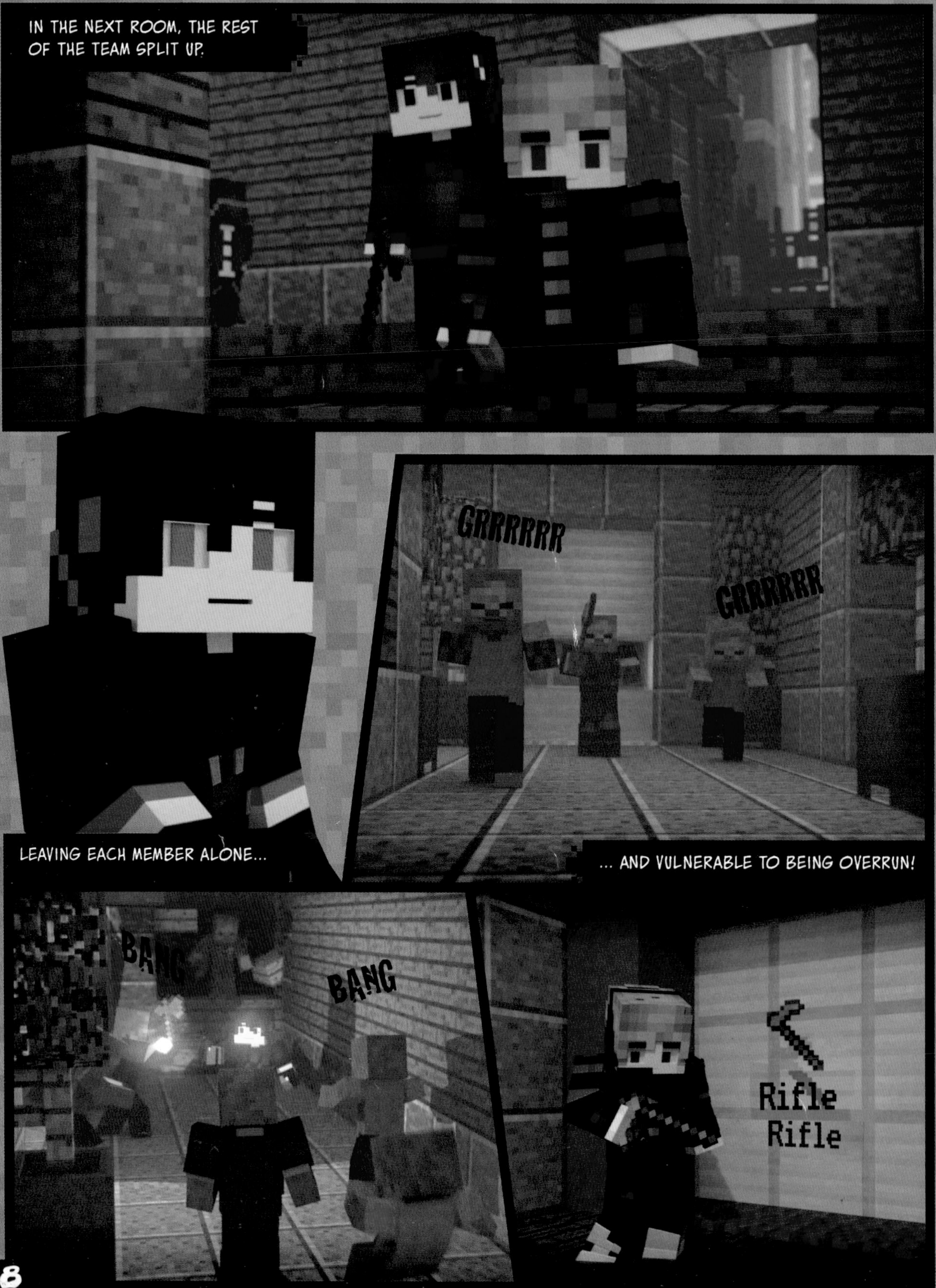
IN THE NEXT ROOM, THE REST OF THE TEAM SPLIT UP.
LEAVING EACH MEMBER ALONE...
GRRRRRR
GRRRRRR
... AND VULNERABLE TO BEING OVERRUN!
BANG
BANG
Rifle
Rifle

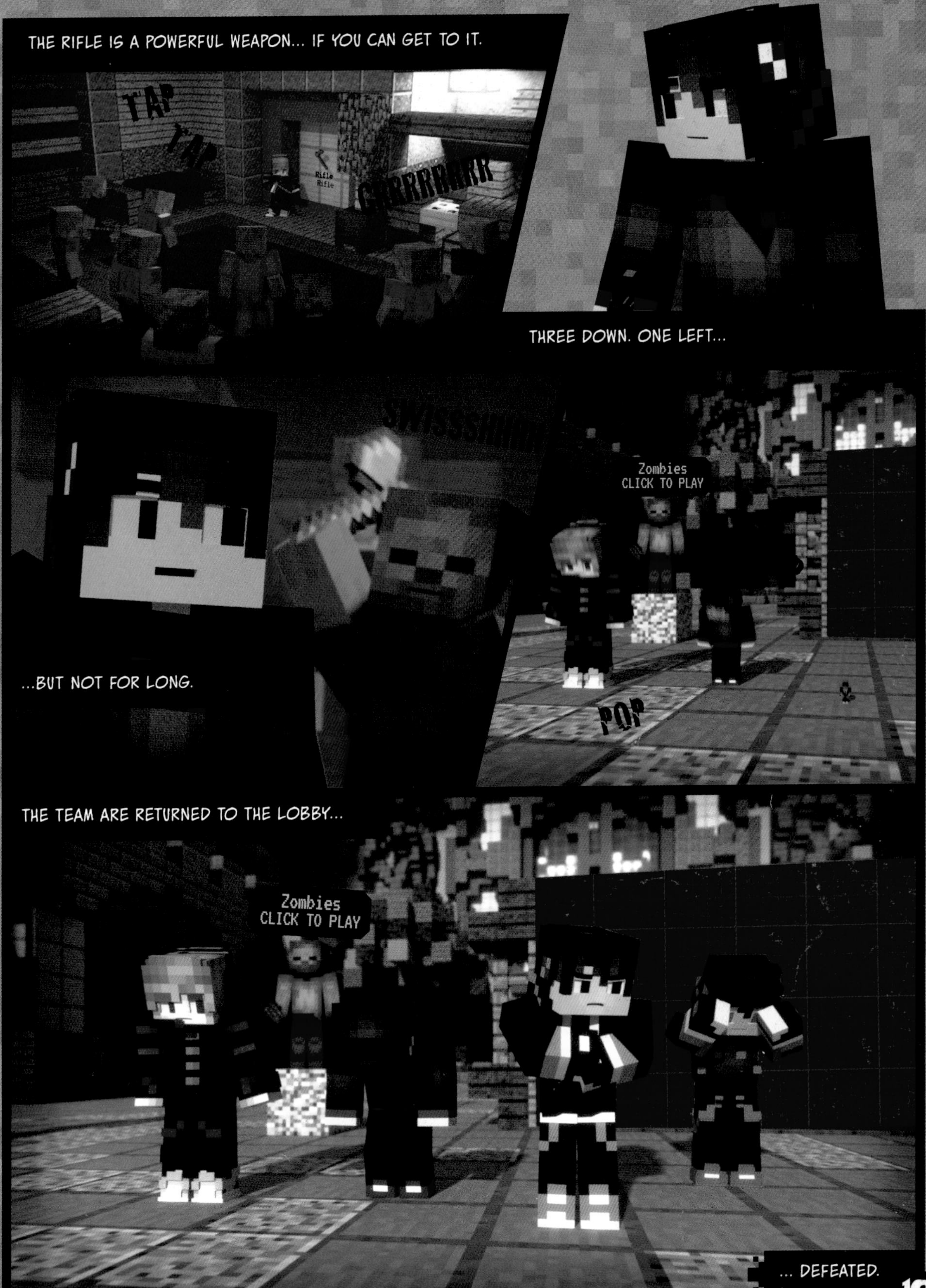
THE RIFLE IS A POWERFUL WEAPON... IF YOU CAN GET TO IT.
TAP
TAP
Rifle
Rifle
GRRRRRRRR
THREE DOWN. ONE LEFT...
SWISSSHHH
...BUT NOT FOR LONG.
Zombies
CLICK TO PLAY
POP
THE TEAM ARE RETURNED TO THE LOBBY...
Zombies
CLICK TO PLAY
... DEFEATED.

THE LOBBY IS THE PLACE TO ACCESS MINIGAMES ON THE HYPIXEL SERVER...

Mystery Vault
RIGHT CLICK

Mystery Vault
RIGHT CLICK

... AND DERP IS HERE TO PLAY!

Zombies
CLICK TO PLAY

NOW ALL HE NEEDS IS SOMEONE TO PLAY WITH HIM.

Zombies
CLICK TO PLAY

LOOKING
4 TEAM

DERP LOOKS AROUND...

... SEARCHING FOR ANYONE TO JOIN HIS TEAM.

LOOKING 4 TEAM

... BUT NO ONE WANTS TO PLAY.

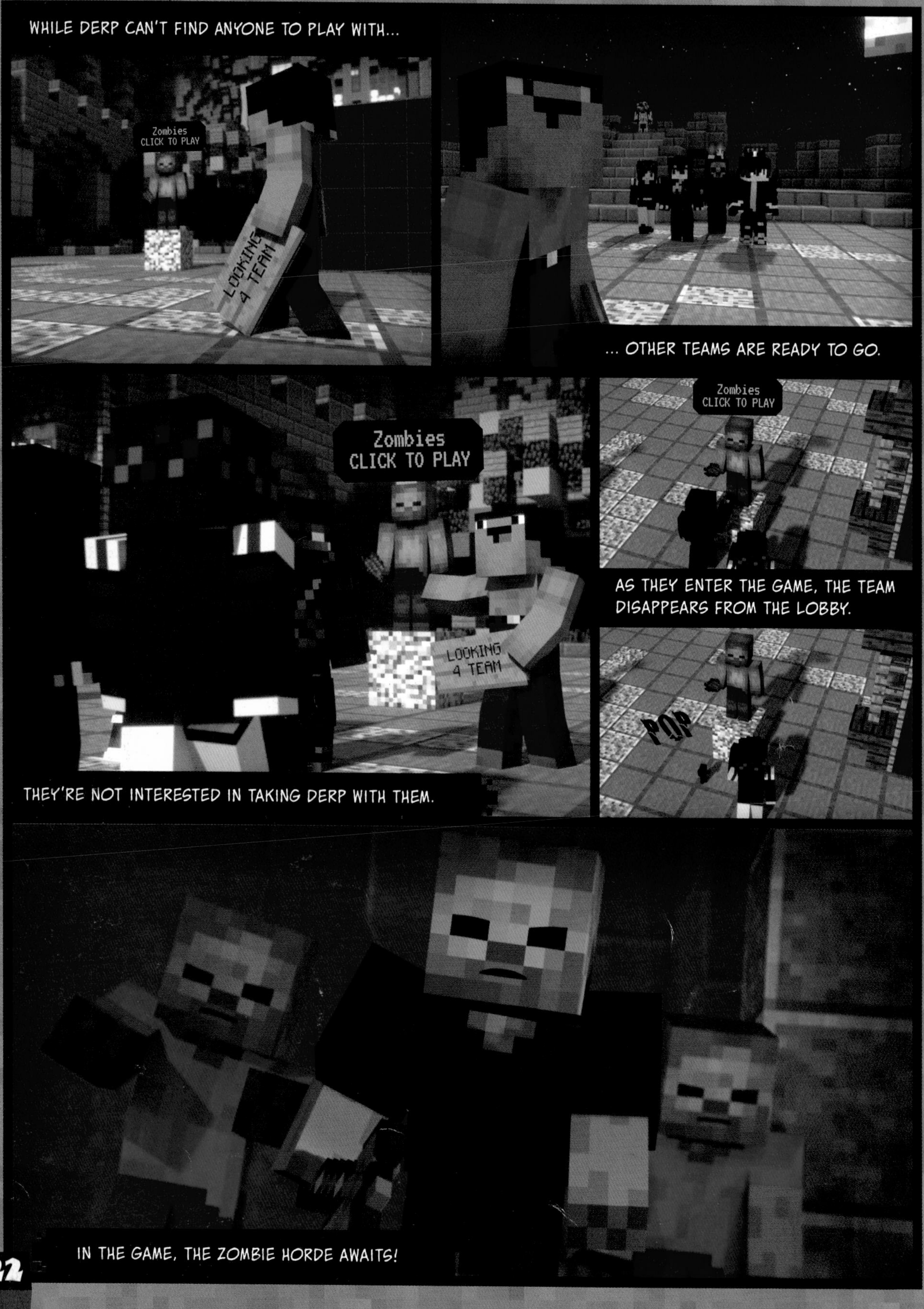
WHILE DERP CAN'T FIND ANYONE TO PLAY WITH...
Zombies
CLICK TO PLAY
LOOKING 4 TEAM
... OTHER TEAMS ARE READY TO GO.
Zombies
CLICK TO PLAY
LOOKING 4 TEAM
THEY'RE NOT INTERESTED IN TAKING DERP WITH THEM.
Zombies
CLICK TO PLAY
AS THEY ENTER THE GAME, THE TEAM DISAPPEARS FROM THE LOBBY.
POP
IN THE GAME, THE ZOMBIE HORDE AWAITS!

BUILDING DEFENCES IS A GOOD START.

BUT WHEN TWO OF THE TEAM TRY TO PLACE THE SAME BLOCK AT THE SAME TIME...

... THEY'RE SO BUSY FIGHTING THEY DON'T SEE THE ZOMBIES COMING!

**POWER SWITCH**
1000 Gold

TO WIN THE GAME, THE TEAM NEEDS TO TURN THE POWER ON.

**POWER SWITCH**
1000 Gold

BUT THEY DON'T HAVE THE GOLD.

DISAGREEMENT LEADS TO RESENTMENT...

**POWER SWITCH**
1000 Gold

... AND A **PIG ZOMBIE** CUTS THEM DOWN WHILE THEY'RE ARGUING.

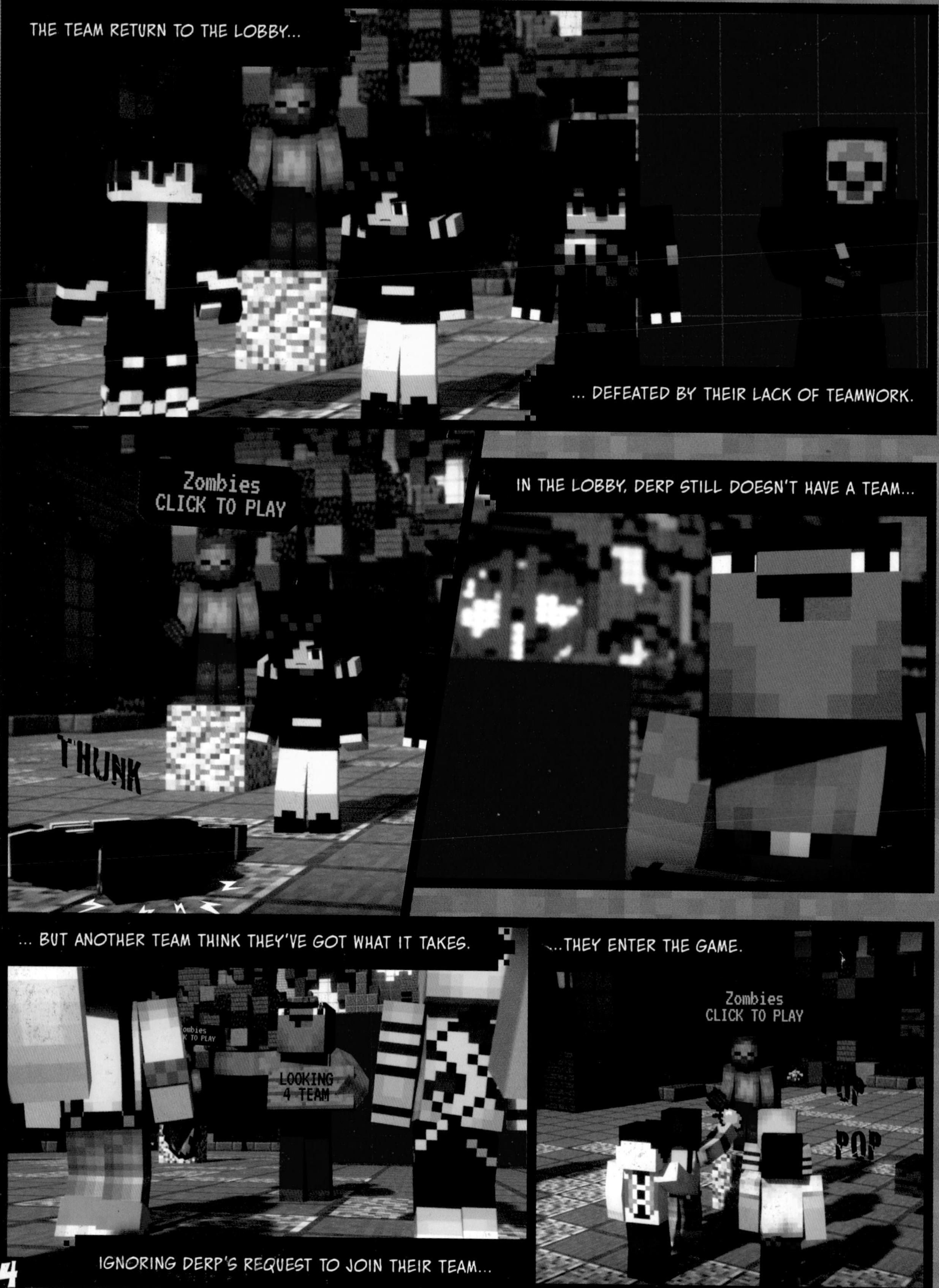
THE TEAM RETURN TO THE LOBBY...
... DEFEATED BY THEIR LACK OF TEAMWORK.
Zombies
CLICK TO PLAY
THUNK
IN THE LOBBY, DERP STILL DOESN'T HAVE A TEAM...
... BUT ANOTHER TEAM THINK THEY'VE GOT WHAT IT TAKES.
LOOKING
4 TEAM
IGNORING DERP'S REQUEST TO JOIN THEIR TEAM...
...THEY ENTER THE GAME.
Zombies
CLICK TO PLAY
POP

IN THE GAME, THREE OF THE TEAM PLAN THEIR STRATEGY...

... BUT THEY DON'T KNOW WHAT TO DO NEXT.

WHILE THE FOURTH MEMBER IS ALREADY RUNNING FROM TROUBLE!

THE REST OF THE TEAM TURN AS HE DASHES IN...

PURSUED BY **BOMBIE!**

PANICKED, HE PILES INTO THE REST OF HIS TEAM...

... AND BOMBIE DETONATES, ENDING THE GAME.

BACK IN THE LOBBY, DERP IS TOO SAD TO EVEN LOOK UP AS THE TEAM REAPPEARS, DEFEATED.

READY TO GIVE UP, HE ABANDONS ANY HOPE OF FORMING A TEAM.

WHAT'S THIS? SOMEONE HAS FOUND HIS REQUEST!

DERP LOOKS OUT INTO THE NIGHT...

ALL ALONE! POOR GUY!

WHO'S THIS? IT'S **THE OLD MAN** BEHIND HIM...

LOOKING
4 TEAM

THE OLD MAN INTRODUCES DERP TO THE
LAST TWO MEMBERS OF THEIR TEAM.

...WITH A REQUEST!

A CUPCAKE...

... AND A TURTLE.

AT LAST, DERP HAS HIS TEAM!

**27**

INSIDE THESE SINISTER HALLS, A NEW GAME OF **ZOMBIES** BEGINS.

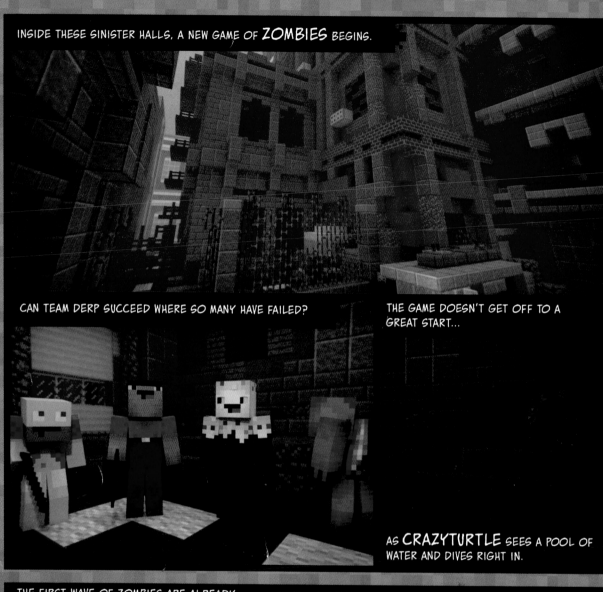

CAN TEAM DERP SUCCEED WHERE SO MANY HAVE FAILED?

THE GAME DOESN'T GET OFF TO A GREAT START...

AS **CRAZYTURTLE** SEES A POOL OF WATER AND DIVES RIGHT IN.

THE FIRST WAVE OF ZOMBIES ARE ALREADY APPROACHING...

AND THE OLD MAN DOESN'T EVEN SEE THEM COMING.

THE OLD MAN IS SHOVED TO THE GROUND.

DERP TURNS AROUND IN TIME...

... TO SEE HIS FALLEN TEAMMATE!

DERP DOESN'T HESITATE.

WHILE CUPCAKE DRAGS CRAZYTURTLE OUT OF THE POND...

... DERP HELPS THE OLD MAN TO HIS FEET.

THE TEAM REGROUPS. IT'S TIME TO PLAN TACTICS!

WORKING AS A TEAM AT LAST, THEY MOVE AS A UNIT.

COVERING EACH OTHER AS THEY BUILD DEFENCES.

FIGHTING THEIR WAY TO THE POWER SWITCH...

POWER SWITCH
1000 Gold

... WITH ENOUGH GOLD TO ACTIVATE THE POWER!

THE TEAM MOVES QUICKLY THROUGH THE WELL-LIT CORRIDORS.

TAKING DOWN WAVES OF ZOMBIES!

REACHING THEIR OBJECTIVES!

DRAWING THE ATTENTION OF A GREATER THREAT...

FWOOOOSSSHHHHH

INFERNO.

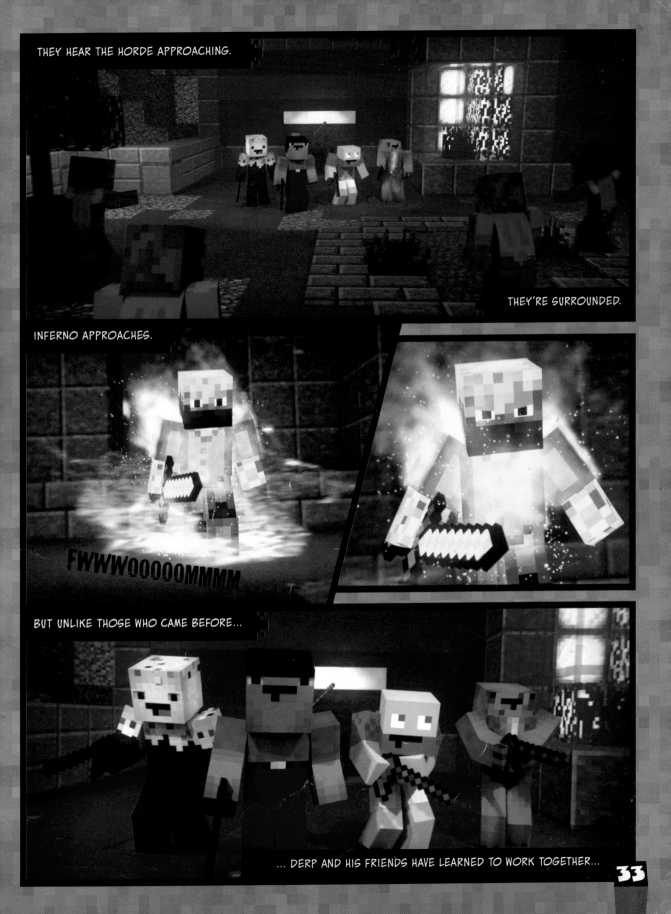

THEY HEAR THE HORDE APPROACHING.

THEY'RE SURROUNDED.

INFERNO APPROACHES.

FWWWOOOOOMMMM

BUT UNLIKE THOSE WHO CAME BEFORE...

... DERP AND HIS FRIENDS HAVE LEARNED TO WORK TOGETHER...

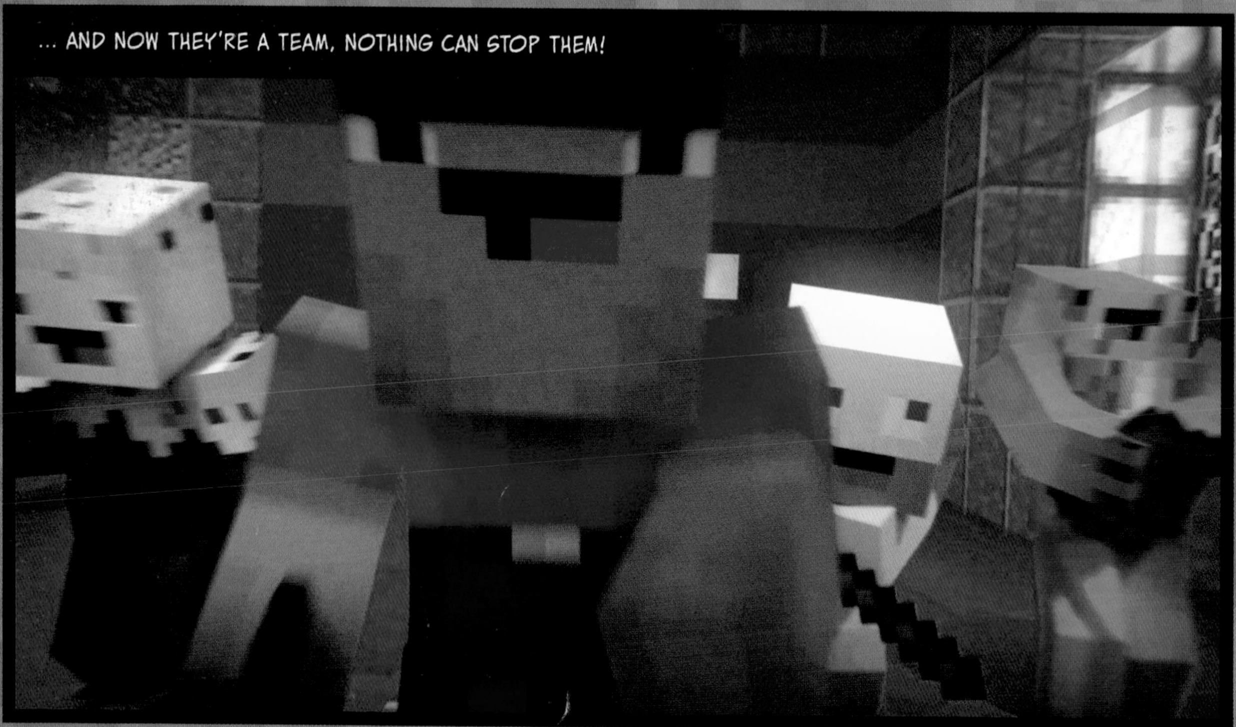
... AND NOW THEY'RE A TEAM, NOTHING CAN STOP THEM!

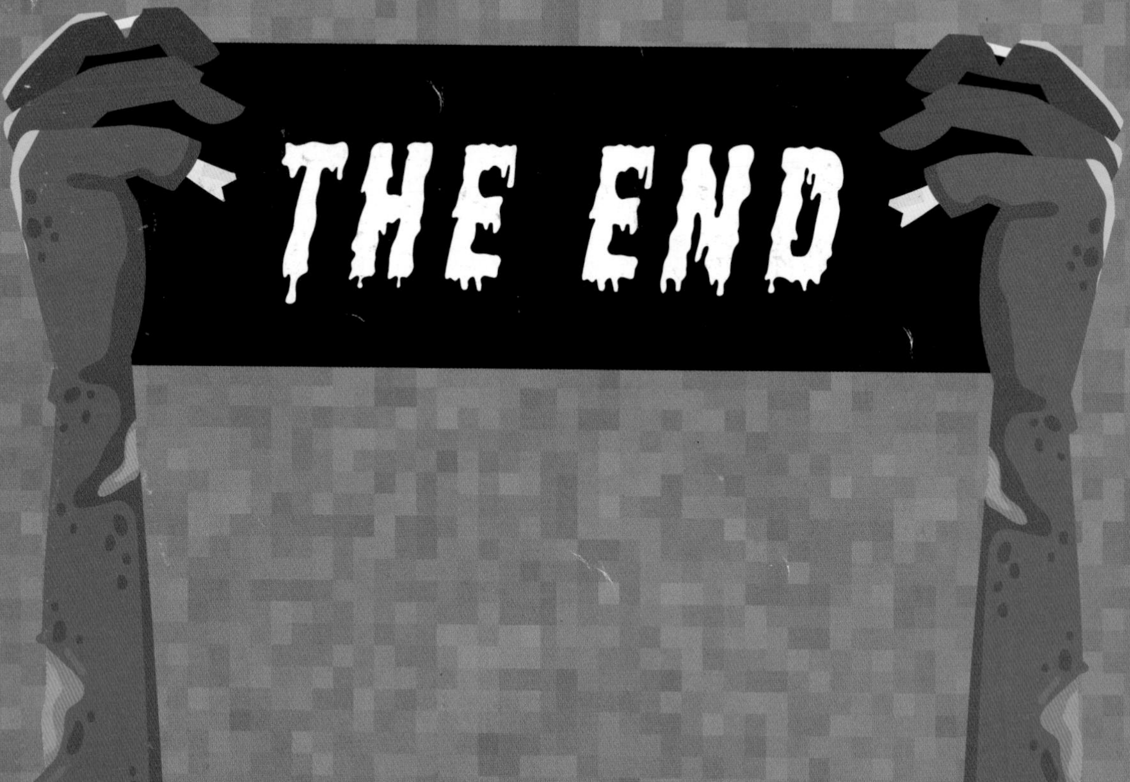
THE END

# GIANT DERP!

IT'S A LOVELY SUMMER DAY IN MATTUPOLIS.

THE PERFECT DAY TO GO TO THE CARNIVAL.

Mattupolis CARNIVAL

DERP IS AT THE CARNIVAL WITH HIS PET FISH.

WHAT COULD GO WRONG?

DERP EXPLORES THE CARNIVAL.

THERE'S MUSIC...

MAGIC...

THE GREAT MAGICIAN
Magic like you've never seen

...GAMES.

THERE'S EVEN SOMETHING THAT CATCHES FISH'S EYE...

SQUID_LORD'S AQUARIUM.

FISH WANTS A GO.

DERP STRETCHES HIS ARM OUT...

... AND THROWS FISH STRAIGHT INTO THE TANK.

FISH SEEMS HAPPY...

SQUID_LORD, NOT SO MUCH!

WHILE THE MAGICIAN PERFORMS...

... FOR AN APPRECIATIVE AUDIENCE...

... DERP IS MORE INTERESTED IN THE CAKE STALL.

... AND DERP GRATEFULLY ACCEPTS ONE.

THE CUPCAKES LOOK DELICIOUS...

WHAT HARM COULD IT DO?

AS A RABBIT APPEARS FROM A HAT...

... CUPCAKES DISAPPEAR INTO DERP.

FISH WANTS A GO.

THE MAGICIAN TELEPORTS FROM ONE DOOR...

... TO ANOTHER.

BUT DERP IS TOO SUGAR-CRAZED TO CARE...

HE EATS ALL THE THE ICE CREAM... THEN THE CANDY FLOSS... SNATCHING TREATS WHEREVER HE CAN!

THIS IS AN UNSTOPPABLE SUGAR RUSH...

CHOMP CHOMP

... AND DERP HAS ONE LAST TREAT IN HIS SIGHTS.

A VERY SPECIAL CAKE ON THE MAGICIAN'S STAGE.

IT SEEMS TO CALL OUT TO DERP...

DERP'S HOPES ARE SHATTERED...

... BUT SECURITY HAS OTHER IDEAS.

... UNTIL HE COMES UP WITH A PLAN.

DERP HIDES UNDER THE BARREL TO SNEAK PAST SECURITY...

... ONLY TO FIND HIMSELF STUCK IN THE BARREL.

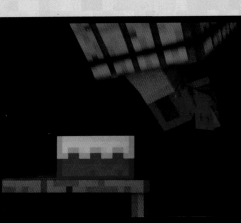

HE MANAGES TO THROW OFF THE BARREL...

... BUT IT KNOCKS THE MAGICIAN OFF STAGE.

... AND WHEN IT LANDS ON THE TABLE IT FIRES A MAGICAL BOLT -

HIS MAGIC WAND IS THROWN HIGH INTO THE AIR...

-. THAT BLASTS DERP ACROSS THE CARNIVAL!

HAVING CAUSED SO MUCH TROUBLE, DERP HEADS BACK OUT INTO MATTUPOLIS.

DERP FEELS SORRY FOR HIMSELF, NOT EVEN REALISING...

... THAT THERE'S MORE TROUBLE TO COME.

BIG TROUBLE.

BIG, BIG TROUBLE!.

DERP'S GETTING BIGGER! HE NEEDS HELP... AND HE KNOWS WHERE TO GET IT.

**... BLACK PLASMA STUDIOS!** IN THESE PALATIAL OFFICES, A HARD WORKING TEAM CREATE SPECTACULAR ANIMATIONS... WHICH ARE THEN ADAPTED INTO BOOKS...

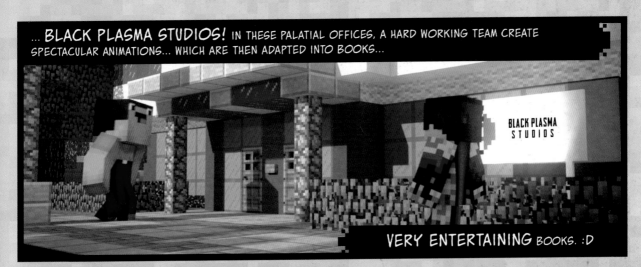

**VERY ENTERTAINING** BOOKS. :D

DERP TRIES TO GET IN, BUT HE'S ALREADY TOO BIG!

HE RINGS THE DOORBELL TO GET THE TEAM'S ATTENTION.

BUT THEY CAN'T HEAR HIM BECAUSE THEY'RE TOO BUSY...

... WORKING? YES. **WORKING**.

NO MATTER HOW HARD HE RINGS, DERP GETS NO ANSWER...

... AND HE'S **STILL GROWING!**

**43**

THE BLACK PLASMA TEAM ARE STILL HARD AT WORK WHEN A SHADOW FALLS OVER THE WINDOW.

A VERY LARGE SHADOW!

COULD... COULD IT BE...?

GIANT DERP!!

PEOPLE FLEE FROM THIS TITANIC TERROR...

... A FRUSTRATED GIANT DERP REACHES FOR THE OFFICE...

... AS THE TEAM FLEE IN FEAR!

GIANT DERP TEARS THROUGH THE BUILDING...

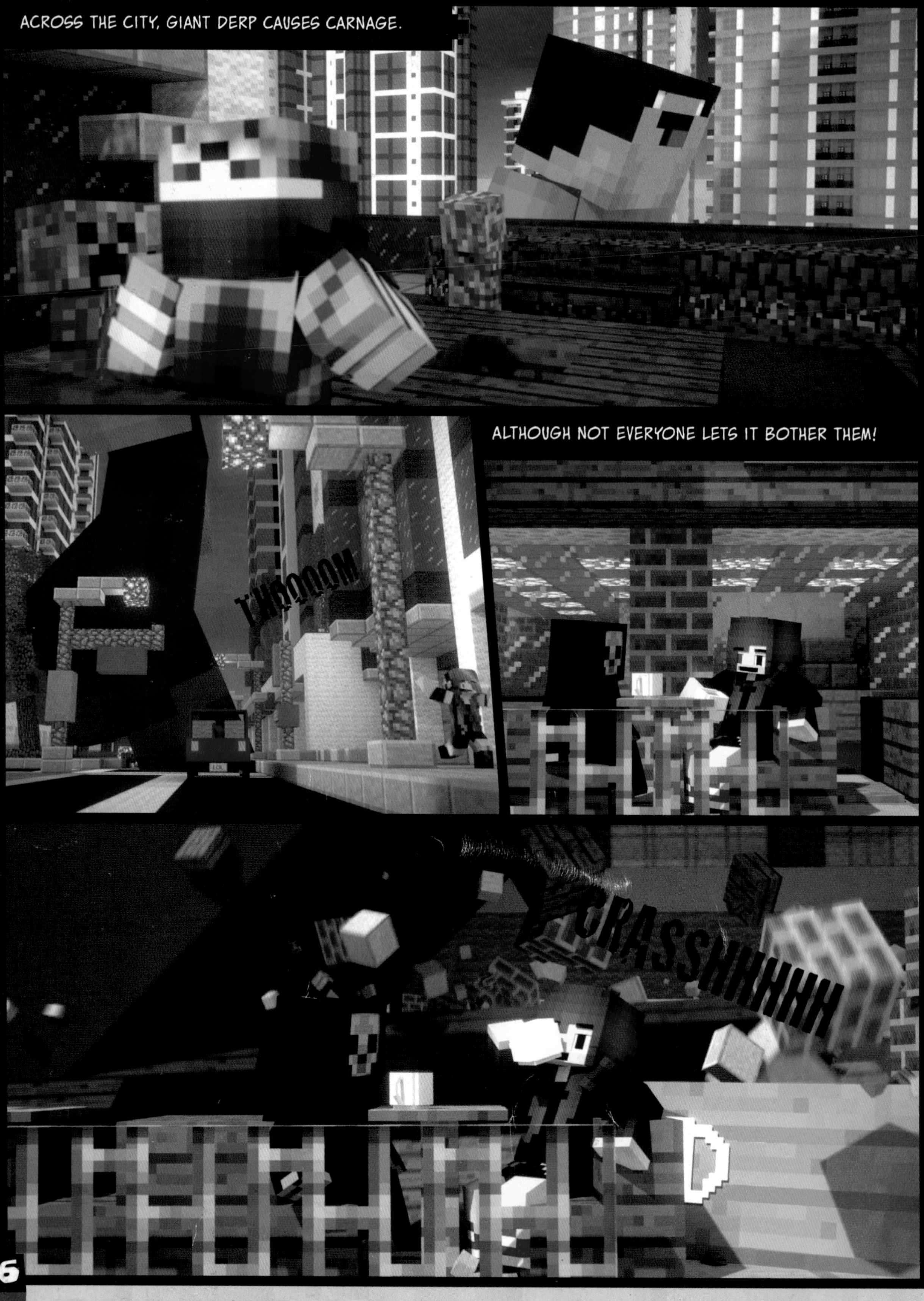
ACROSS THE CITY, GIANT DERP CAUSES CARNAGE.
THOOOOM
ALTHOUGH NOT EVERYONE LETS IT BOTHER THEM!
CRASSHHHHHH

GIANT DERP'S RAMPAGE HAS NOT GONE UNNOTICED.

THE NEWS HELICOPTER MOVES IN FOR THE PERFECT SHOT.

BOX
96
2:39pm

**BREAKING NEWS**
**GIANT DERP WRECKING CITY!**

DERP SWATS THE HELICOPTER
OUT OF THE SKY!

WHILE MOST OF THE CITIZENS FLEE, OTHERS HEAD TOWARDS GIANT DERP...

VRRRRRMMMMMMM!

KER-KLUNK!

... AND THEY'RE HERE TO DO MORE THAN TAKE PICTURES.

BANG BANG

AS DERP IS ATTACKED FROM BELOW...

PLUNK

... HE'S ALSO ATTACKED FROM HIGH UP.

THE BOW IS AN ELEGANT WEAPON...

PLUNK

... OTHER WEAPONS HAVE LESS CLASS.

RATTTATT

THERE'S ALWAYS AN EVEN BIGGER GUN!

THE ROCKET STREAKS THROUGH THE AIR...

FWOOOOSHHH

... IT'S A HIT!

RUMMMMBBLE

RUMMMMMBBLE

BOOM

DERP IS TAKING HITS...

... BUT THEY'RE NOT EVEN SLOWING HIM DOWN!

THUMP

PERHAPS A MORE DIRECT ATTACK WILL WORK?

...NOPE.

AIR SUPPORT SWOOPS IN...

... AS DERP RETURNS TO THE CARNIVAL.

THE MAGICIAN DESPERATELY SEARCHES FOR A SPELL...

WHILE THE LATEST DEFENDERS OF MATTUPOLIS PREPARE TO DROP IN.

A DISTRACTION COMES FROM ABOVE...

RAAATTAAATAATTT

THE MAGICIAN IS ABOUT TO CAST HIS SPELL...

SLAAAP

... BUT FISH LEAPS TO DERP'S DEFENCE, KNOCKING THE MAGICIAN ASIDE!

ONCE MORE, THE WAND SAILS THROUGH THE AIR...

... AS GIANT DERP LOOMS ABOVE.

THE WAND IS CAUGHT BY A DOLPHIN...

... WHO LAUNCHES A MAGICAL BLAST AT DERP.

THE EFFECTS ARE... UNEXPECTED...

ZWEEEEEEK

... FOR ALL CONCERNED.

THE TURTLE THINKS IT CAN DO BETTER...

... TURNING DERP INTO A... DOOR?

IF AT FIRST YOU DON'T SUCCEED...

ZWEEEEEEK

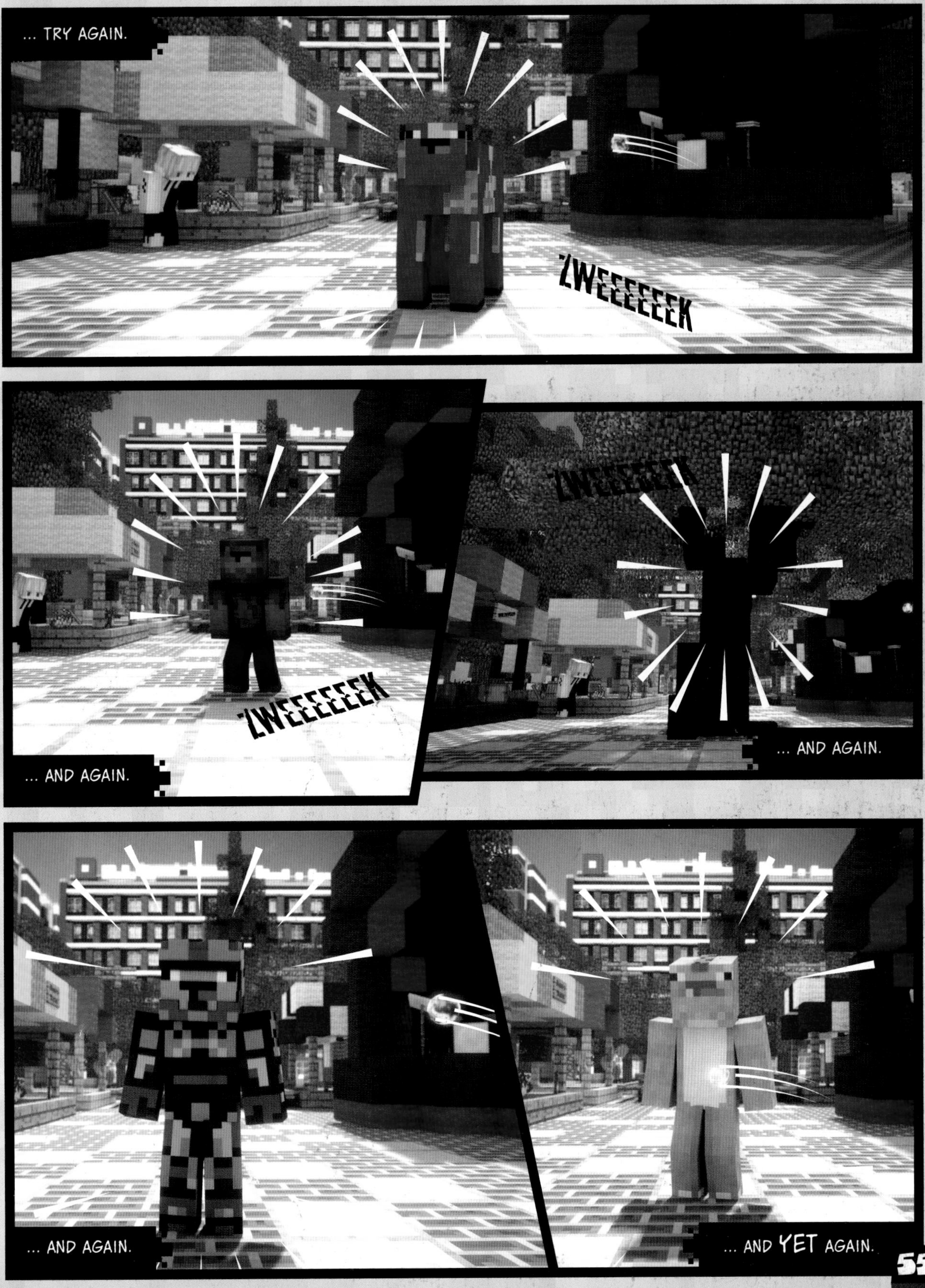
... TRY AGAIN.
ZWEEEEEEK
... AND AGAIN.
ZWEEEEEEK
ZWEEEEEEK
... AND AGAIN.
... AND AGAIN.
... AND YET AGAIN.

FINALLY DERP IS RESTORED TO HIS NORMAL SELF...

... AND DUCKS BEFORE HE CAN BE TRANSFORMED AGAIN.

THE MAGICAL BOLT RICOCHETS...

THE GREAT MAGICI

agic like you've never se

... HITTING THE MAGICIAN HIMSELF.

DERP FINALLY GETS THE CAKE HE WANTED, AND THE WAND...

... FOR AS LONG AS HE CAN STAY AHEAD OF THEIR NOW-TINY OWNER!

# THE END

# NEW HOUSE

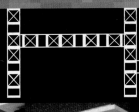

IN THE AFTERMATH OF GIANT DERP'S RAMPAGE...

BLACK PLASMA STUDIOS LIES IN RUINS.

WHAT WILL THE TEAM DO NOW?

AS NIGHT FALLS, THE TEAM ARE LEFT HOMELESS.

THEY'RE TOO DEPRESSED TO EVEN NOTICE A FAMILIAR FIGURE WALKING PAST...

.. UNTIL A MAP FALLS AT SAM'S FEET.

A MAP THAT **MIGHT** BE THE KEY TO SOLVING THEIR PROBLEMS.

THE MAP LEADS TO A BEACH OUTSIDE THE CITY.

NEAR THAT BEACH, THE TEAM FIND...

... AN ABSOLUTE DUMP?

THIS FEELS LIKE A CRUEL TRICK.

RUMMMMMMBBBBLLLE

BUT WHAT'S THAT SOUND?

A TANK ROLLS ON TO THE SITE...

RUMMMMBBLE

... AND BLOWS THE OLD RUIN TO PIECES!

BOOOOOOOM

AS THE SMOKE CLEARS, THE TEAM WONDERS...

... WHO IS THIS MYSTERY VANDAL?

WHO ELSE?!

DERP HAS GATHERED THE TEAM HERE...

... BECAUSE HE HAS A PLAN.

SAM DOESN'T KNOW WHAT TO MAKE OF THIS.

IT LOOKS LIKE A LOT OF WORK FOR FIVE PEOPLE.

BUT DERP HAS THAT COVERED TOO.

HE'S BROUGHT SOME FRIENDS TO HELP.

IT'S TIME TO GET TO WORK!

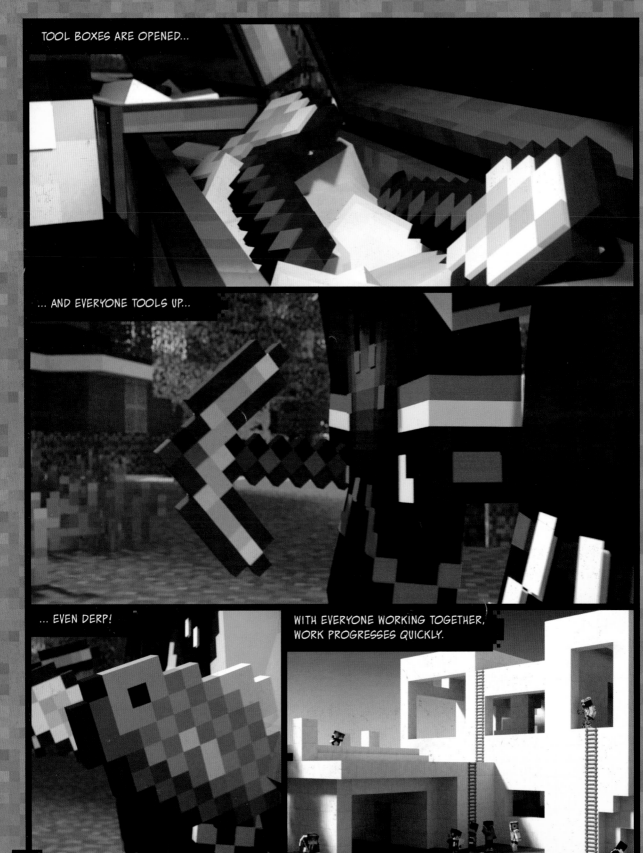

TOOL BOXES ARE OPENED...

... AND EVERYONE TOOLS UP...

... EVEN DERP!

WITH EVERYONE WORKING TOGETHER, WORK PROGRESSES QUICKLY.

EVERYONE HAS THEIR PART TO PLAY.

AS THE SUN SETS, A **SPECTACULAR** NEW BLACK PLASMA STUDIOS OFFICE EMERGES ON A HILLTOP!

IT'S A NEW DAY, AND THE NEW HOUSE IS OPEN FOR BUSINESS!

IT HAS EVERY POSSIBLE LUXURY, FROM A HELICOPTER PAD...

... TO A POOL.

HAVING WORKED HARD, THE BLACK PLASMA STUDIOS TEAM AND THEIR SUPPORTERS KICK BACK...

... AND ENJOY THE RESULTS OF THEIR HARD WORK.

WHILE EVERYONE ELSE HAS FUN...

... A LONE FIGURE STANDS OUTSIDE.

DERP'S DONE WHAT HE SET OUT TO DO.

HE HAS REPLACED THE HOME THAT HE DESTROYED.

AWW. WHERE WILL HE GO NOW?

SAM EMERGES TO FIND DERP OUTSIDE...

... AND INVITES HIM IN.

DERP IS DELIGHTED. AFTER ALL...

... WHAT COULD GO WRONG? :D

# THE END

- TINY DERP -

IN THE NEW BLACK PLASMA STUDIOS OFFICE BUILDING...

CRASH

DERP IS PLAYING IN HIS ROOM.

HE'S DISTURBED BY A NOISE THAT SHAKES THE WHOLE BUILDING.

OUTSIDE, PEOPLE ARE COMPETING ON THE STRENGTH TESTER MACHINE.

PLAYERS BRING THE HAMMER DOWN AS HARD AS THEY CAN.

KLANG

EVERY BLOW OF THE HAMMER SHAKES DERP'S ROOM!

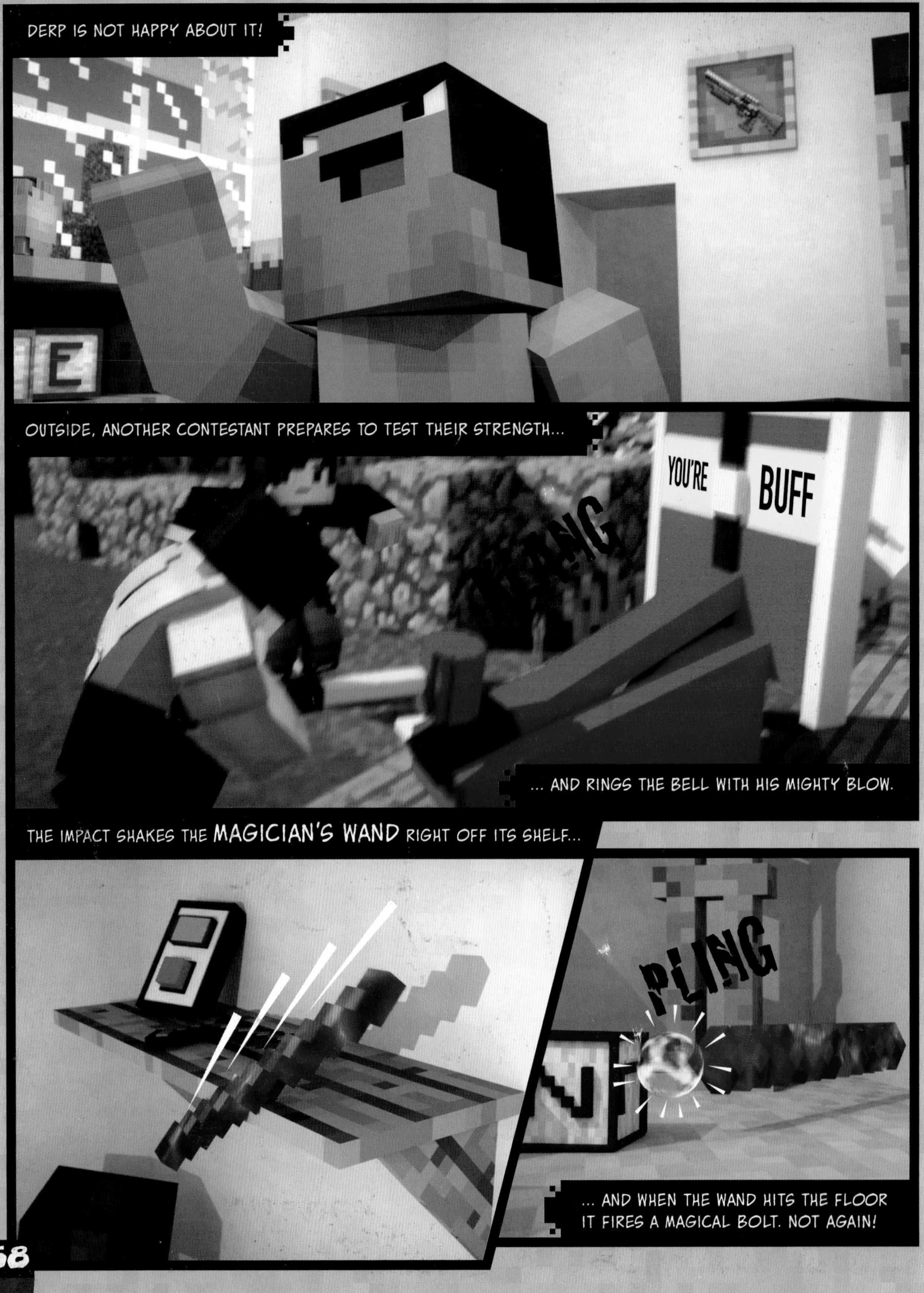
DERP IS NOT HAPPY ABOUT IT!
OUTSIDE, ANOTHER CONTESTANT PREPARES TO TEST THEIR STRENGTH...
YOU'RE
BUFF
... AND RINGS THE BELL WITH HIS MIGHTY BLOW.
THE IMPACT SHAKES THE MAGICIAN'S WAND RIGHT OFF ITS SHELF...
PLING
... AND WHEN THE WAND HITS THE FLOOR IT FIRES A MAGICAL BOLT. NOT AGAIN!

WHERE'S DERP NOW?

UH-OH...

HE'S TINY! NOW EVERYTHING SEEMS HUGE.

FORTUNATELY, THE WAND IS STILL NEAR.

TINY DERP DASHES FOR THE WAND...

SOMETHING THAT LOOMS OVER TINY DERP!

... ONLY TO BE OVERTAKEN BY SOMETHING BIGGER.

ROOOOOWWWWRRRR

DISTRACTED, THE PUG RUNS AWAY...

... TAKING THE WAND WITH IT!

... BUT HIS LEGS ARE TOO SHORT. HE'S EXHAUSTED!

THUD

THUD

TINY DERP CHASES THE DOG...

...HE HEARS SOMEONE COMING...

... IT'S **SKYFALL**.

SQUEAK.

DERP JUMPS UP AND DOWN, DESPERATE TO BE SEEN...

DERP

DERP

... GETTING THE ATTENTION OF SKYFALL'S **BAT**!

THE BAT SWOOPS DOWN TOWARDS TINY DERP...

... WHILE THE DOG GETS AWAY WITH THE WAND.

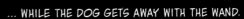

NO ONE CAN CATCH IT NOW!

**71**

WHAT'S THIS, SWOOPING THROUGH THE CORRIDOR?

SQUEAK!

TINY DERP STEERS HIS NEW MOUNT TOWARDS THEIR PREY...

... IN HOT PURSUIT OF THE WAND.

SKYFALL HAS HAD STRANGER DAYS AT THE OFFICE...

... BUT NOT MANY!

TINY DERP HAS NEARLY CAUGHT UP...

... BUT IS **BATTED** BACK!

THE DOG SLIPS INTO THE OFFICE OF HIS MASTER...

IT'S A FUNNY LOOKING STICK...

... THOMAS.

... BUT THERE'S ONLY ONE REASON A DOG BRINGS YOU A STICK.

TO THROW IT FOR THEM!

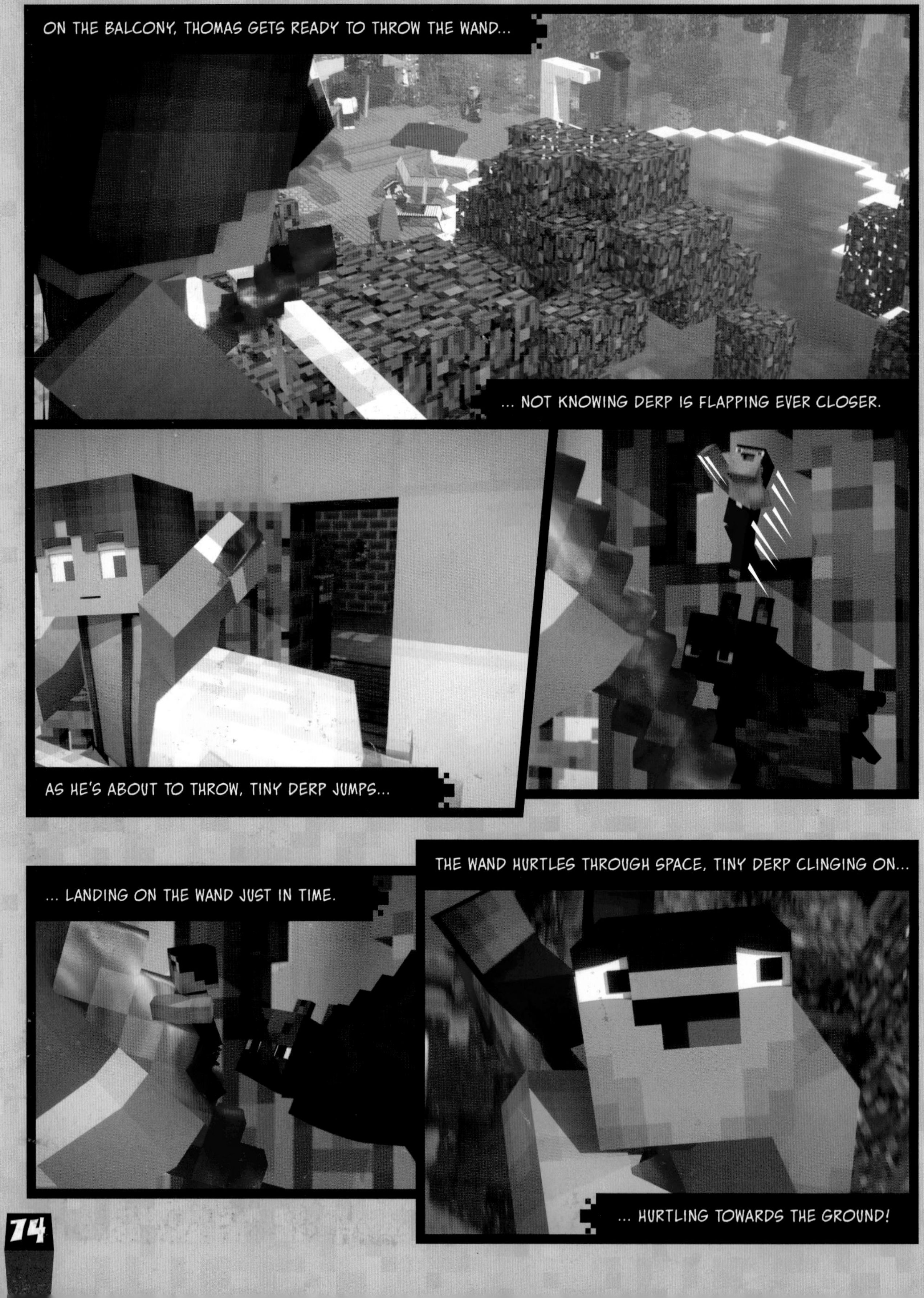
ON THE BALCONY, THOMAS GETS READY TO THROW THE WAND...
... NOT KNOWING DERP IS FLAPPING EVER CLOSER.
AS HE'S ABOUT TO THROW, TINY DERP JUMPS...
... LANDING ON THE WAND JUST IN TIME.
THE WAND HURTLES THROUGH SPACE, TINY DERP CLINGING ON...
... HURTLING TOWARDS THE GROUND!

DERP LOSES HIS GRIP...

... AND THE WAND LANDS, BOUNCES OFF A RUBBER RING...

... AND RICOCHETS TOWARDS THE BARBECUE, DERP SPINNING BESIDE IT.

BOOOIIING

WHILE THE WAND PUSHES ASIDE A BARBECUE FORK...

... DERP MAKES A SOFTER LANDING... ON A SIZZLING HOT STEAK!

PEOPLE ARE HUNGRY, IT'S TIME TO SERVE UP.

THE WAND IS GRABBED AND USED TO SHOVEL...

... ONE STEAK, WITH MEDIUM RARE DERP!

THE FORK BARELY MISSES TINY DERP.

IS HE DOOMED TO BE LUNCH?

DERP JUMPS JUST IN TIME.

A DERP DOESN'T MAKE A GOOD SNACK, AND A WAND DOESN'T MAKE A GOOD FORK.

DERP JUMPS ON THE WAND ONCE MORE...

... AS IT'S TOSSED AWAY.

AGAIN.

... AND BACK INTO THE HOUSE.

BOIIING

BOUNCING ACROSS THE GARDEN...

IN THE HOUSE, DERP FALLS OFF THE WAND...

... AND LANDS IN THE TRASH.

DERP DRAGS HIMSELF UP TO FIND HIMSELF...

... IN THE GAMES ROOM!

THE TRASH TOPPLES OVER...

... AND DERP LANDS GRACEFULLY ON THE FLOOR.

78

MEANWHILE, IN THE STREET OUTSIDE, A TINY FIGURE DRAGS A **SPELL BOOK** TOWARDS THE HOUSE.

BACK IN THE GAMES ROOM, TINY DERP CLAIMS THE HIGH GROUND.

CLIMBING ON TO A TABLE.

FROM HERE HE CAN SEE THE GAME ON SCREEN...

... AND THE KITCHEN AREA WHERE... WHAT'S THAT?

... THE PLAYERS...

THERE IT IS!

**79**

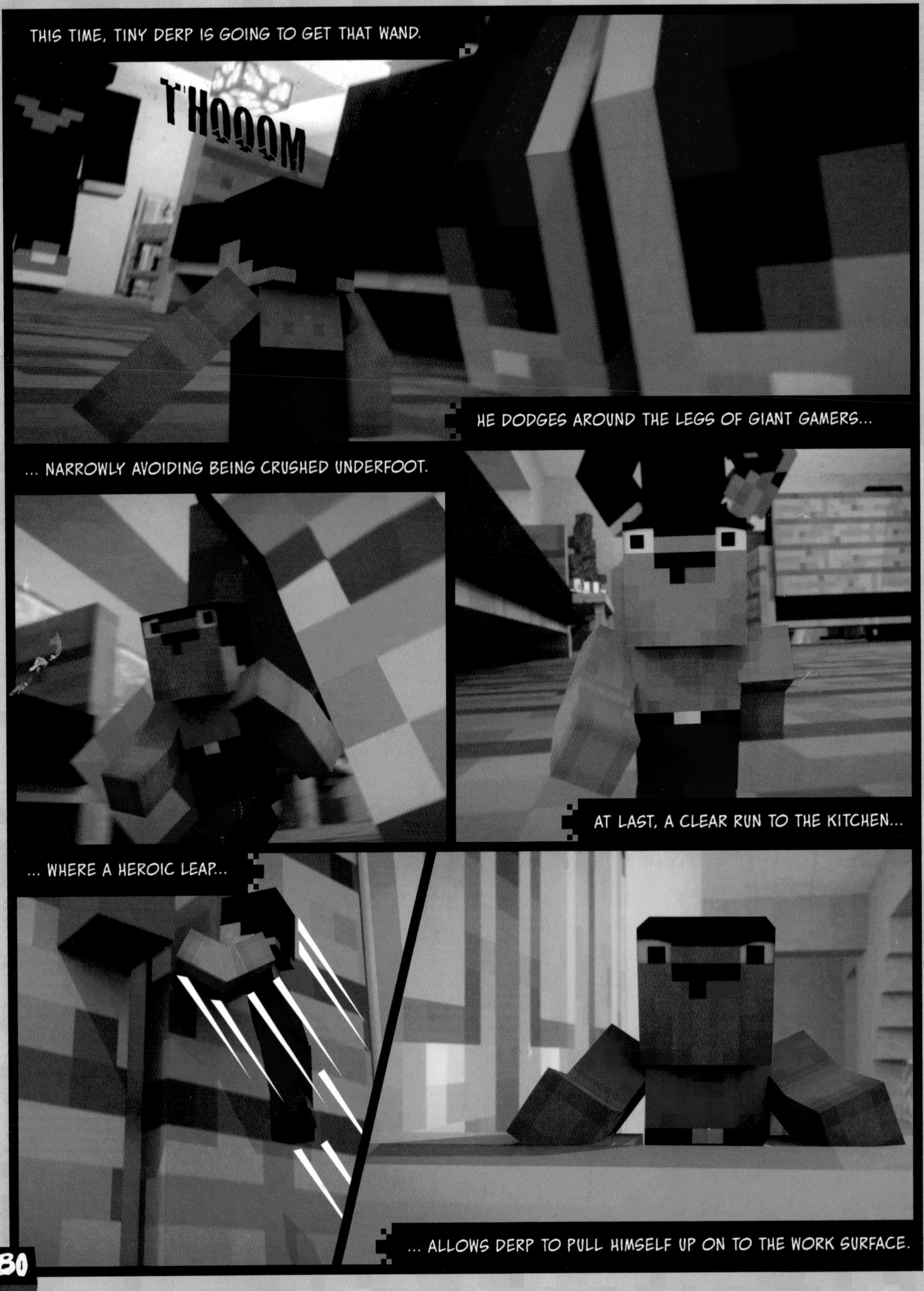
THIS TIME, TINY DERP IS GOING TO GET THAT WAND.
THOOOM
HE DODGES AROUND THE LEGS OF GIANT GAMERS...
... NARROWLY AVOIDING BEING CRUSHED UNDERFOOT.
AT LAST, A CLEAR RUN TO THE KITCHEN...
... WHERE A HEROIC LEAP...
... ALLOWS DERP TO PULL HIMSELF UP ON TO THE WORK SURFACE.

FROM DERP'S POINT OF VIEW, ITS A BIG LEAP FROM THE WORK SURFACE TO THE TABLE.

UNLESS...

DERP RUNS TO THE TOASTER...

... LINES IT UP...

... AND PREPARES FOR LAUNCH!

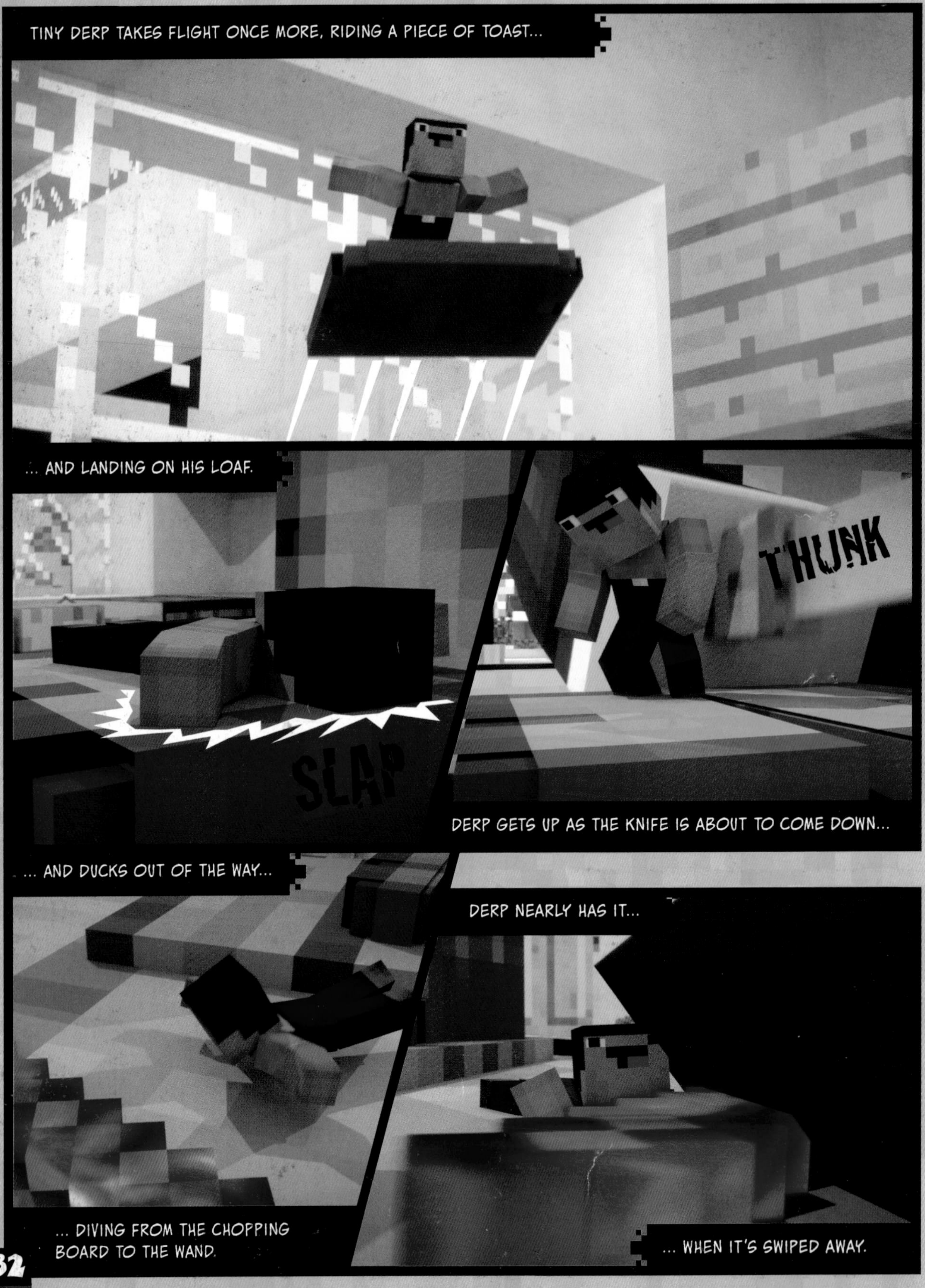
TINY DERP TAKES FLIGHT ONCE MORE, RIDING A PIECE OF TOAST...
... AND LANDING ON HIS LOAF.
SLAP
THUNK
DERP GETS UP AS THE KNIFE IS ABOUT TO COME DOWN...
... AND DUCKS OUT OF THE WAY...
... DIVING FROM THE CHOPPING BOARD TO THE WAND.
DERP NEARLY HAS IT...
... WHEN IT'S SWIPED AWAY.

THE WAND MAKES FOR A HANDY TEA-STIRRER...

... BEFORE BEING ABANDONED ONCE AGAIN.

MEANWHILE, **THE MAGICIAN** HAS NEARLY COMPLETED HIS LONG JOURNEY.

BLACK PLASMA
STUDIOS
OFFICE BUILDING

ALL HE NEEDS TO DO IS REACH THE DOORBELL.

INSIDE, DERP RUNS FOR THE ABANDONED WAND.

SURELY THIS TIME HE CAN REACH IT?

NEARLY THERE...

GOT IT!

ALAS, FOR A TINY DERP...

THE WAND IS JUST TOO HEAVY.

84

AS TINY DERP WONDERS WHAT TO DO, **KNIGHT** APPROACHES...

DERP WANTS KNIGHT TO USE THE WAND ON HIM.

... AND CAN'T QUITE BELIEVE WHAT HE'S SEEING.

SAM'S NO MAGICIAN, BUT GIVES IT A TRY.

NOTHING.

BING BONG

SOMEONE'S AT THE DOOR.

KNIGHT FINDS A TINY MAGICIAN CLINGING TO THE DOORBELL...

... AND HE'S BROUGHT JUST THE BOOK TO PUT THINGS RIGHT.

NOW KNIGHT HAS EXACTLY WHAT HE NEEDS...

... TO RESTORE HIS TINY FRIENDS TO THEIR NORMAL SIZE.

TWO WAVES OF THE WAND...

OFFICE BUILDING

ZEEEP-ZEEP!

... AND ALL IS AS IT SHOULD BE.

WHILE DERP CHECKS ALL HIS BODY PARTS ARE THE RIGHT SIZE...

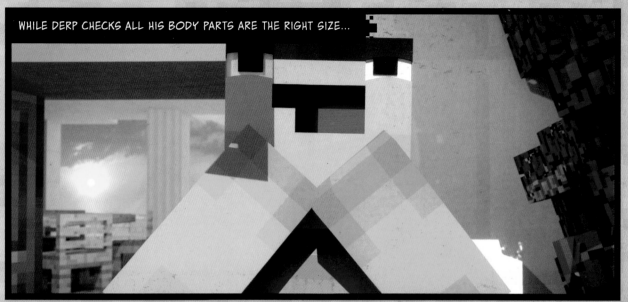

... KNIGHT GIVES THE SPELL BOOK AND WAND BACK TO THEIR RIGHTFUL OWNER!

DERP, HOWEVER NEVER LEARNS.

THE MAGICIAN IS HAVING NONE OF IT.

POOR DERP. HE JUST WANTS A LITTLE MAGIC OF HIS OWN...

... AND GETS IT, HIS VERY OWN MAGICIAN'S HAT.

IT'S A HARMLESS ENOUGH GIFT... RIGHT?

BACK IN HIS ROOM, DERP REACHES INTO THE HAT AND PRODUCES...

... A FISH!

THEN... THREE FISH!

DERP HAS AN IDEA.

FISH EVERYWHERE!!

SCHLOOOPPPP

CRRRASSSSSSHHHHHRPPP

MORE FISH!!

THE END

ON A SNOWY WINTER'S DAY, ALL IS QUIET AROUND THE LITTLE COTTAGE.

# CHRISTMAS DAY

INSIDE, DERP WAS ASLEEP... TO BEGIN WITH.

HE'S WOKEN BY A KNOCKING AT THE DOOR...

OUTSIDE, A VERY SPECIAL MESSAGE AWAITS DERP ON THE MAT...

BPS
Christmas
Invitation

... AN INVITATION TO THE **BLACK PLASMA STUDIOS** CHRISTMAS PARTY.

DERP KNOWS EXACTLY WHAT TO DO.

HE'S GOING TO BAKE THE **PERFECT CAKE.**

... INGREDIENTS.

CAKE RECIPE

3 milk

3 wheat

1 egg

2 sugar

FIRST THINGS FIRST...

MILK, EGGS, SUGAR, WHEAT.

LUCKY FOR DERP, THESE INGREDIENTS...

... ARE ALL AROUND HIM!

AFTER SOME HIGH-SPEED FARMING...

MOOOOO

CLUCCCKKK

DERP HAS WHAT HE NEEDS.

LET'S BAKE!

SIZZZLE

PLINK!

DERP COMPARES THE CAKE HE'S MADE...

... TO THE ONE HE WANTED TO MAKE...

... AND FINDS HIS LACKING.

THE CAKE IS REJECTED... VIA THE WINDOW.

DERP DOES NOT GIVE UP THAT EASILY.

DERP GATHERS HIS INGREDIENTS ONCE MORE...

... AND TRIES AGAIN.

MOOOO

SIZZZLE

DERP CAN HARDLY BREATHE IN ANTICIPATION.

PLINK

DERP TAKES HIS OWN FAILURE... POORLY.

CRASSSSHHH
THUMMMP

DERP DESPAIRS. WHAT WILL HE BRING TO THE PARTY IF NOT A CAKE?

WAIT! THAT'S PERFECT.

DERP RUSHES INTO ACTION.

CHOPPP
CHOPPP

AT LAST, HE'S READY FOR THE PARTY.